SPACE BOY

and His ~~Sister~~ Dog

Dian Curtis Regan

Illustrations by
Robert Neubecker

Boyds Mills Press
An Imprint of Highlights
Honesdale, Pennsylvania

For Steve, who helped me find Planet Home
    —DCR

For Isidore
    —RN

Text copyright © 2015 by Dian Curtis Regan
Illustrations copyright © 2015 by Robert Neubecker
All rights reserved.
For information about permission to reproduce selections
from this book, contact permissions@highlights.com.

Boyds Mills Press
An Imprint of Highlights
815 Church Street
Honesdale, Pennsylvania 18431

Printed in Malaysia
ISBN: 978-1-59078-955-1
Library of Congress Control Number: 2014943969

First edition
Production by Margaret Mosomillo
The text of this book is set in Billy.
The illustrations are done digitally.
10 9 8 7 6 5 4 3 2 1

1. A New Mission

Niko lives on Planet Home
dog, Tag, and his copilot, Radar.

Niko is the captain of his very own spaceship.
He built it all by himself.

Niko's sister, Posh, lives on Planet Home, too.
But she is not in this story.

Niko and his copilot search for their next mission.

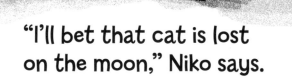

"I'll bet that cat is lost on the moon," Niko says.

"Start the engines, Radar. We will find it!"

2 To The Moon!

The spaceship blasts off from Planet Home. It zips to the moon.

After landing, Niko discovers a stowaway.

Posh is **not** supposed to be here. She is **not** in this story.

3. LOST CAT

Back at the spaceship,
Posh finds Tag's doggie treats.

She sprinkles treats
on a moon rock.

But Posh is not in this story.
Let's get back to Niko and his crew!

With Radar's help, Niko and Tag search the top of the highest moon mountain.

No cat.

They search the bottom of the deepest moon crater.

NO CAT!

They ask the Man in the Moon. The Man in the Moon says,
"The cat went thataway!"

They search thataway.

No cat.

ARF! ARF!

Finally, Niko and his crew give up. Niko feels sad. He cannot find the poor cat.

Tag does not feel sad at all. He did not want to find the cat. He just wanted to run and bark all over the moon.

4. FOUND CAT

Niko, Tag, and Radar go back to the spaceship.

Posh is sitting on a moon rock.
She is petting the lost cat.

Since Posh is not in this story,
it is SO NOT FAIR that she found the missing cat.

The cat has gobbled up all of Tag's doggie treats.
Tag is not a happy dog.

"I am going to keep the cat I found," Posh declares. The cat begins to purr.

Radar feels like purring, too. Secretly, he likes cats better than dogs.

5. HOMEWARD BOUND

Tag is not happy to see a cat boarding the spaceship.
Niko is not happy to see a sister boarding.

"You cannot keep the cat you found," Niko tells Posh. "She belongs to Mrs. Jarabaldi, and you know it."

"Okay," Posh says. "I will return her when we get back to Earth."

"No!" cries Niko. "*I* will take the cat back to Mrs. Jarabaldi. *You* have to stay on the moon."

6. LOST SISTER

The spaceship blasts off. Niko watches his sister grow smaller and smaller.

"Warp speed, Radar!" Niko says. But Radar is ignoring Niko because Niko left Posh on the moon.

"Doggie treats?" Niko asks Tag. But the bag of treats is empty. Tag refuses to stay in the copilot seat with Radar.

Niko tries to pet Mrs. Jarabaldi's cat,
but she won't let him.

Niko feels lonely.

"Radar! What is our next mission?"
Radar doesn't answer, but Niko knows what he is thinking:
There seems to be a sister lost on the moon.

Niko does not like it when his crew ignores him.
"Okay, then," he says with a sigh. "We will find her."

Niko turns the ship around. Radar fires the engine.
Tag leaps into the copilot seat.
Mrs. Jarabaldi's cat climbs onto Niko's lap and begins to purr.

This time, *Niko* finds the one who is lost on the moon. Now Posh *is* part of this story. "I am a space hero!" Niko cries.

He tries to rescue the lost sister, but the lost sister refuses to be rescued.

8. HOME IN TIME FOR DINNER

The spaceship blasts off once more.
It zips across the sky.

And they all fly back
to Planet Home for supper—

except for Posh,
who finds her own way home.